Four Winds Press, Macmillan Publishing Company, 866 Third Avenue, New York, NY 10022.
Maxwell Macmillan Canada, Inc., 1200 Eglinton Avenue East, Suite 200, Don Mills, Ontario, M3C 3N1.
Macmillan Publishing Company is part of the Maxwell Communication Group of Companies.
First published in Great Britain in 1993 by Andersen Press Ltd., London.
First American edition 1993.
Color-separated by Photolitho AG Offsetreproduktionen, Gossau, Zürich.
Printed and bound in Italy by Grafiche, AZ, Verona.
10 9 8 7 6 5 4 3 2 1
Library of Congress Cataloging Card Number 93-9410
ISBN 0-02-726361-4

# KING
## OF THE WOODS

by David Day

illustrated by Ken Brown

Four Winds Press ❊ *New York*

Maxwell Macmillan Canada   *Toronto*
Maxwell Macmillan International   *New York   Oxford   Singapore   Sydney*

It all began early one morning when a little Wren flew out
into the middle of a forest clearing and found a golden apple
sitting on top of an old stump.

The little Wren landed next to the big, juicy apple.

She was about to peck it when a Crow flew up and landed
on the other side of the apple.

"I'm the king of the woods," cawed the Crow grandly, as he puffed his chest up to twice its usual size and chased the little Wren off the stump. "And I'll take this apple as my prize."

It was a silly boast. Even the frightened little Wren knew that as she flew off into the trees. But Crows like to brag a lot to make themselves feel important.

Still, it would have been wiser had the Crow not boasted so loudly. For just as he was about to eat the golden apple, an Eagle swooped down and knocked the Crow right off his stump.

The Crow may be able to bully little bush birds, but the Eagle was not having any bragging bird claiming to be lord of his forest.

"I am the king of the woods," screamed the Eagle, perched on the stump in the clearing. "And I'll take this apple as my prize."

But, even for the Eagle, it would have been wiser not to
have boasted so loudly. For just as he was about to pick up
the golden apple with his talons, a Wolf rushed into the
clearing. Seeing the fierce animal running toward him, the
Eagle fled.

The Eagle may be the king of birds, but the Wolf was not having any bragging bird claiming to be lord of his forest.

"I am the king of the woods," snarled the Wolf, standing next to the stump in the clearing. "And I'll take this apple as my prize."

But, even for the Wolf, it would have been wiser not to have boasted so loudly. For just as he was about to take a bite out of the golden apple, a Bear rushed into the clearing. Seeing the ferocious beast running toward him, the Wolf fled.

The Wolf may be master of his pack, but the Bear was not having any bragging dog claiming to be lord of his forest.

"I am the king of the woods," roared the Bear, sitting next to the stump in the clearing. "And I'll take this apple as my prize."

But, even for the Bear, it would have been wiser not to have boasted so loudly. For just as he was about to grab the golden apple with his paw, a Bull Moose rushed into the clearing. Before the Bear could move, the mighty Bull Moose scooped him up in his huge antlers and threw him into the air.

The Bear may be a terror to other animals, but the Bull Moose was not having any bragging beast claiming to be lord of his forest.

"I am the king of the woods," bellowed the Bull Moose, standing next to the stump in the clearing. "And I'll take this apple as my prize."

This time, nobody else entered the clearing, because the Bull Moose really was the biggest and strongest animal in the woods.

The Bull Moose was so sure of himself that he bellowed even more loudly: "Is there anyone who dares to challenge the king?"

All was silent, but just as the Bull Moose was about to bite into the golden apple, a shrill, little voice piped up.

"I will challenge you."

It was the little Wren.

The other animals could not believe their ears or eyes.
If the Bull Moose had not been such a grumpy beast, he
probably would have laughed. Instead, he snorted and
pawed the earth.

Then the Bull Moose charged straight at the little Wren.

In return, the little Wren charged straight at the Bull
Moose.

Just as they were about to collide, the little Wren flew right up the Bull Moose's nose.

The Bull Moose stopped in his tracks.

He shook his head until his ears flapped. He banged his nose on the ground. He rattled his antlers against some saplings. But he could not get the little Wren out of his nose.

The Bull Moose got madder and madder as the Wren pecked away with her sharp, little beak at the inside of his big, soft nose.

The Bull Moose became so angry that he charged at the trunk of a huge tree with all his might

and knocked himself out cold.

"I am the king of the woods," chirped the little Wren in her boldest voice, as she stood on the stump in the clearing. "And I'll take this apple as my prize."

None of the other animals dared to approach.
All about the clearing they watched in silence
while the mighty king of the woods
climbed up on top of the golden
apple and ate her lunch.